CHRISTINE POWER
Illustrations By: Presea Reed

My Talking Pets

iUniverse books may be ordered through booksellers or by contacting:

iUniverse
1663 Liberty Drive
Bloomington, IN 47403
www.iuniverse.com
1-800-Authors (1-800-288-4677)

ISBN: 978-1-6632-0418-9 (sc)
ISBN: 978-1-6632-0419-6 (e)

Library of Congress Control Number: 2020912147

Print information available on the last page.

iUniverse rev. date: 07/28/2020

This book is dedicated to all the boys and
girls who have ever had a pet, wanted a pet,
or has plans to get a pet someday.

My dogs name is Chopper.

This is Stormy my sisters cat.

These are my moms birds Pretty and
Brute. Here are my talking pets.

They don't actually talk. Not like you and I talk to each other. They talk in their own way. When they stand by the door they are saying they want outside.

Chopper scratches his food bowl when he is hungry. When he wants his bone he jumps up and down wagging his tail and barking. That is how I know he wants his bone.

Chopper talks to me in his own way.

Other animals have a way of letting
you know what they want also.

When I yell "hungry" for chopper to come
eat, Stormy comes running too.

Brute reminds me that he is hungry by banging
his food dish on the inside of his cage.

When the sun shines through the windows,
the birds sing to let us know they like it.

Animals communicate in different ways.

Look around when you're out taking a walk, or visiting a relative or friend.

You will begin to see pets and animals everywhere talking by wagging their tail or whinning.

Some animals flick their ears, others twitch their noses.

Chopper gets excited when I say "walk" because he loves to go for a walk in the park. He always makes me feel loved and needed. I want him to feel as loved and happy as he makes me feel.

I started with easy words like his name.

Use
words
like
"NO"
"DOWN"
"OUTSIDE"
"INSIDE"
"HUNGRY"

Chopper knows that "STAY" means to stay put.

And "Down" means to get down.

Sometimes I have to tell him twice.

You can use words besides hungry, like
"CHOW"
"DINNER"
"EAT"
You can even make clicking sounds or just whistle.
They will come running for dinner time.

Your pet learns faster and better if you use the
same command each time, and keep it simple.
I feed Chopper at the same time
everyday, this is good for his diet.
It's also good because he never lets me forget he is hungry.

Chopper thanks me by licking me.

Don't forget to let him outside, or take him for a walk after your pet is through eating OR wakes up from a nap.

One time I forgot to let him outside after dinner, so he went to the bathroom on my mom's favorite rug.

She was mad at both of us.
It's easy to remember.
Outside after eating.
and
Outside after a nap

My mom buys Chopper bones so he
wont chew on everything.

One time he chewed one of my mom's gray slippers.

Chopper is so cute when he is in trouble.

Sometimes he flips onto his back and
curls up while wagging his tail.

Don't forget to let your pet know when
he is being good as well.

You can give them a treat when they are good.

The only time I use two words is for good
girl, bad girl, good boy, bad boy.

When Stormy jumps onto moms birdcage, Mom yells "NO"

Stormy understands she's in trouble and runs.

The best part of having a pet is when you first come home after you were gone for awhile. They are so happy to see you. Snuggles are great too, and so is having a best friend by my side.

Chopper and I talk to each other all the time. He
understands me and I understand him.

You can understand your pet too, if you just LISTEN.

So you see, my pets DO talk to me!

Printed in the United States
By Bookmasters